Buzzing Like a Bumblebee

Heli Susanna Katajamäki

ETHENE

Isokyrö 2023

COPYRIGHT © Heli Susanna Katajamäki & Ethene Ltd 2023
Title: Buzzing Like a Bumblebee
Original title: Pörriäisen surinoita
Publisher: Ethene oy, Isokyrö, Suomi-Finland, www.ethene.eu
Author: Heli Susanna Katajamäki
Translator: Susanna Rönn
Illustrator: Heta Kettunen

ISBN 978-952-65083-2-0 (pocket book)
ISBN 978-952-65083-0-6 (hardcover)
ISBN 978-952-65083-1-3 (PDF)
ISBN 978-952-65068-8-3 (EPUB)
ISBN 978-952-65068-9-0 (kindle)

First Buzzes

Thank you to Mom and Dad,
my dear parents

It's time for life, it's time for loves
it's time for youthful loves
it's time for adulthood loves
it's time for old age loves

There are times, there are ways
always suitable
the kind that are needed

As long as you open your heart
you receive
you are a friend to others

Heli Susanna Katajamäki (born Lähteenmaa)
In Isokyrö on August 15, 2022

Contents

Wingstroke

That time when I set out
I rose with purely paperless wings
up to laugh, learn
seek
and find I did

My find I had to bury
without questioning
not out of internal compulsion
though that turned out to have been part of the reason

I replaced my wings
I mounted ironclad ones
I bridged the time
I resisted the supply
I received the little that was on offer
and so it came to
holding yet another funeral

I fixed my wings
though without band aids
Not wanting to believe at all
for the one I had met to long for a butterfly
A butterfly I am only when soaring
worldlessly
but I am starting to believe
that a bumblebee with tens of minor cuts and bruises
will also do

I buzz into my flower

A Bumblebee's Oath

Though I am just a little bumblebee
I have buzzed among alien species
spread useless weeds
wasted energy on uselessness
been the exception proving the rule

If I am good enough for you
I promise to hum in you
without sparing my energies
loyally
like a soldier of the fatherland
until my strength runs out
or death breaks me down into dirt

And if my humming dies down before you
I promise that even from above
I'll hum to you
if not in my own voice
through the humming of others
until we are both done making war

Solely from My Soul

I had to age
many annual cycles
live half of my life
to see myself
to understand
my tenacity
the ceaseless fluttering of my wings
even after
the ground has shaken
the numerous times my shanks
snapped

I guess you still doubt
which is understandable not knowing my soul
we've only just embarked upon our maiden voyage

But don't doubt it
when I say
now I know myself
and have never buzzed my oath to anyone but you

Will you trust me rightnowatthisverymoment?
I feel lonely still

A Wonderful World

If you already listened to me buzz
you may keep doubting
I confess
that faced with this miracle
I too am humble

Can a soul identify a soul
maybe not as the only possible
but the only suitable one
in this moment
in this time

I wish to believe
I wish to hope
I wish to love
I wish
That is enough for me
What about you?

The Stupidity of a Stupid Bumblebee

What kind of a stupid bumblebee male
would not understand his own good
receive the love
of a female
offering it with a sincere heart

Luckily my chosen male
is smart
perhaps smarter than me
And he is
I know it
and is not
I know it too

Different meadows grow different flowers

Visible on the Surface

I used to swim under the surface
It suited me
I didn't see the surface
I didn't feel its vibrations
I didn't miss the surface tension under my feet
I was not familiar with the phenomenon

The water darkened in places
The bottom goo tempting me to sink
A deadhead got in my way
I swerved kept swimming
it might have been impossible alone

I persevered
I kept breathing
Everyday close to everfrost
my life was
the slapping of the tail
partly to fulfill the fate
of my very own

The bubbles on the surface gave me away
The net in disarray
still I got pulled up
how will I ever learn to breathe on the surface
forced penned to something new one can restart

Briefly to whizz
not avoiding accidents
until I found the seeker
without realizing it at first

Suddenly I am in the moment
you are in the moment
we are in this life

Ha ha

I'm too old to be flying in the mist
I think I've always been
and so have the end results:
the male did not commit
Did I push too much? Buzz too much? Buzz too little?
Not feeling like a queen now
What if
I vibrated in the morning, what would you do, and
cleaned out the nest?

If I vibrate,
will you be too busy to send a single message
aren't you feeling anything or is it just me and my feelings
are you seeing others, which would keep you missing
do you get that my fire is burning, I can't wait for long for yours
to start
how have you made your previous relationships work
or have you and I guess you have
to hug, kiss, make love, I'm a little busy, I'm so
old and even in that case we could go our separate ways if
that's the consensus

Do you have a master plan or are you just a bit slow
and if you are slow, is it fixable by any chance?
Here I am taking a flight
Even if tied to my apron strings
the last thing you'd have to worry is
that you wouldn't do for me

Is there another reason or am I not the right one for you?

A Melancholy Flight

My bumblebee is not coming, reaching out
not when I'm waiting or even
when I've been waiting for long

The moment we locked eyes
feeling the warmth of your smile
is fading away

Nosediving into the ground
with a crash
without caring why
caring why this way

I have learned to survive
bumps, blows, deaths
but right now they're fading into memories

When again your invisibility, quietness
have me turning on the waterworks
once more it was nothing but a daydream
In my lonesome loneliness
I pupate
when I recover from the crash
When

Humorless Daydreamer

That's me
Maybe I was whizzing too fast
but that's my way to fly
I was trying to say why
I like to give things a fair try

I have whizzed and flown before
I have crashed
oftentimes tens of times
believing in the other one
making myself believe that it's fine
coming up with excuses for them

And in the world at large
in the big picture
it does not matter

But my heart
is dying piece by piece
I'm crying a cry
that cleanses
as soon as I understand
as soon as you understand
no more
Over

All or nothing
Now: nothing

Our Love Is War

My melancholy fades away for a moment
when I realize
that almost and not just almost
this is the war I want

I want to be able to talk
about bygone wars
I want to be able to talk
about bygone policies, concessions
negotiations
And why I am now compelled to stand
by my policy
why it is worth going to war
if only for a miniscule cell in the nest

But it is my cell
If I don't go to war now
I am already losing my footing
and when I now go
I can gain my footing
in you

For love grows deeper by fighting
small battles
Kissing and making up can be sweet

If we don't get there
there was never one drop of seriousness
I do have a backup strategy
to cover the losses:
simply to reconstruct other
nests of mine

I'm not going to lose the war in advance
There is no need for that
because in the name of fairness I must confirm/confess
that my male is no Putinist; neither a dictator nor a torturer
Yet it is obvious that he did not understand me
why the matter is important

There's an explanation for that too:
he's yet to understand
how to take my feelings into account
that I don't have my whole life to wait
for him to grow up and start feeling
I'm buzzing into battle!
Veni, vidi, vici

I'm a Greedy Little Bumblebee

I have calmed down
my fruitless fussing has stopped
I am sorry
that I didn't immediately realize
but I haven't
because you offered me no help
You already believed for the both of us

I'm taking pleasure in resting
waiting for you
Day and night still
you are working carrying honey
But when the carrying is done
energies restored
I know
you're coming

I'm excited
I/You would buzz if I/you passed
Before that we
keep buzzing flying humming

And innovating!
Together we look in the mirror
If we see our crooked noses
let it be our strength
Although you get to be my master
and the architect of our lives
you'll also learn from me
like I will from you
We will get exponentially stronger

I/You need you/me
I/You love you/me
My/Your soul is open for you/me

The Unbearable Difficulty of Agreement

What if my bumblebee sent me a message tomorrow
I'm thinking
Once again I'm having to remind myself
of trusting him
I must trust
give him some time
presume innocent unless life proves otherwise
Impossible, trust is in us

But I intend to keep schooling him
Bringing up at the very least
our inferior skill of agreement

We have agreed on a time
but we haven't defined it in precise terms
I could show him a bit of affection
when I have only just identified the lack of indefinability
as the root of the problem

How can we buzz on in a way
to learn together without lots of drama?
I guess it is to anyone's advantage
to live life by beautifully buzzing and loving away from the
theatrics

Drama might come in handy but it always takes energy
Maybe especially because of my male's busyness
I will start by thanking for the answer
lightly remarking on the flaws in the agreement
and end by telling about my longing

Oh how lovely it is to hum my drama in my head and to share
it
to all of you

To let it out in poetry
all the while developing my skills at understanding love
and tomorrow in real life I will be able to spur on the two of us
buzzing together

The finish line is getting close: the race is about developing
ourselves against ourselves
We will win this thing!

As a Matter of Fact

A poet I may be
a fine buzzer, keeper of the narrative tradition
yet like a bolt out of the blue
I realize the extent of my stupidity
Might my male also be stupid?

There was also no definition in our agreement
of taking the initiative
there was clarity only in terms of vibrating

Although I am clear on the principle of a buzz for a buzz
as a practice it is an agreement only for those who adopt it
Who waits and why?
What are his parents like toward him?
Accepting, caring, seeing
or none of the above?

Ambition and pushing oneself always stem from somewhere
Self-control may extend to all areas of life
messaging
frugality
with so much to do one might deny desire altogether

Maybe I am sidetracked
My curiosity has been awakened
How to awaken his?
Perhaps I won't respond until he does. I won't
But if we ever meet again
my questions seemingly carefree
will serve a purpose

A Researcher's Touch

I must admit
I was schooled on males by a male
who reacted to my humming
my agreeing
my profound reflecting
my feelings with a pass

Did he take a pass on me too
by keeping to the point
as a professional should

Yet we're not in a professional relationship, not even a
honeyed one
and couldn't be
because God created the male mainly for mating

I am fine with mating
as long as feelings are involved
Do those humming the richness of their feelings feel more than
those hiding them?

Even this aspect I can understand
while descending to the same level of humming and ascending
I will study this

Runny Eyes

Suddenly my mind goes to a sick bumblebee
whom I got to know in a paperless world
I am in the moment in the nest in limbo close to the sea
when the light came closer at a moment of departure
maybe it was him, as it wasn't my father, my first worry

I don't know
maybe not I hope I'm only a bit confused
But it does not do me good, affects my happiness
The lack of your protection feels like a sick pain
worsened by my illusion about you as a violator
who has left the path of support for one of vengeance
or a vantage point at least

Vengeance might be an exaggeration
careful consideration
to cover one's back
you must know too

But could we make one thing clear?
Remember
if you use your will to school me
never do it when you are hurt

Schooling is forbidden when hurt
no matter who is doing it
In its place help the other one understand
why you are feeling what you are
Meet the other one by humming until you drop
we'll pick you up later on
Let love soften your head

It's unnecessary to be hurt by a network of assumptions
that relies on the free flow of thoughts
That's not to claim these lessons as bottomless
relationships stratify through generations

And then there is this fact: every moment compounds turn into
substanceless souls

I might have given you too good of an edge
It's just that I've never understood
why one should hold back on feelings of love
because if anyone wrongfully uses that
they can hold a mirror up to them

On the Ability and Need to Buzz

Wouldn't it be easy
if the other one could verbalize it:
I'm still pondering it considering this
it's a big decision and we will or won't move on

It would eliminate all the useless musings
Allow me to ponder return from my fantasies to reality
all at once

As such pondering is a sign of conscientiousness
of taking things seriously
But I keep vibrating
about the many relationships ripped into pieces mid-flight

For what's equally clear is
that like all other forms of anxiety
insecurity bursts out as flames or fury or at the very least
a fit of anger
that is fueled by insecurity
Life is a journey on the continuum of polarization
the insecure one chasing the elusive one

And the paradox of it!
The infatuation can make the elusive one anxious
especially if the timing is not right for them
But remember then to live in the moment
because anxiety will not change things
in the past or future
no more than the agony of guilt does

Nor does infatuation equal commitment
it's brain fog of things to come
and so the main thing to consider is
whether you want to keep going

Why on earth is it so
that it's the opposites that attract?

There is still hope for all
in every relationship
when you memorize my TSU model:
Give **T**ime
Give **S**pace
Try to **U**nderstand

I think I'll tattoo that on my front shank

In Anxiety

If I had realized
that finding true love is this much work
I might have skipped the whole thing
How I admire you my hard-working bumblebee
that despite realizing it
you did your homework, looked for instructions, science-based
if not quite scientific, and kept trying
Boy do I like those who try!

Yet I must buzz my own viewpoint:
if I understood what and why we are moving ahead like this
I'd exhaust myself less
I'm assuming we're doing this together toward togetherness
Faith and hope are not always easy to keep up
This little bumblebee is melancholy again

On the other hand this is just fine
I got to experience the entire emotional scale from uncertainty
to expectation
What would falling in love be without anxiety?
Too sensible, boring fermenting

Still my conscience is making me ask
are you completely sure?
Give it more thought
You don't yet know
the whirlwind you're about to dip your feet in

It revolves around its axle with increasing speed
until it falls down to get up
except for the last time

But don't you worry
you can count on me
It just doesn't keep me from sniping at you a bit
just for the hell of it
in case it could pull you up in the mouthparts

I promise not to tease you too much, meet you halfway or
even more
although I might sometimes fly off the handle
Because I understand you:
it is not easy to live
with your self-control pressing into your parts

Maybe!

Now I might know
how to handle you
but if my assumption is wrong
we are fucked
for my approach will always be wrong

Instead I should put my velvet gloves on
but I don't feel like it at all
But what would be a greater irony of fate than
kind of starting over

Is there any possibility
for us to rely on pure facts
with raw honesty
without sparing each other
revealing our innermost selves to each other

If you didn't see it yet
will you watch the movie with me?
Or do you ignore my feelings and wishes?
I'm already growing smaller
But I will stick to my choices
let this be my destiny

I still trust my intuition
I believe in my dreams
for I only dream of things
that lead to good results

My mind is blowing
The burning question anywhere in the world is what your
childhood was like, how your mother nurtured you, how your
father treated you, how you did in school, or youth, or the
loves of your life?

Do hum
I will
listen

Maybe I will make it with this solution
as I let go of my gigantic expectation
Maybe we are meant
to remain unknown to each other for substanceless times
To reveal each other only in part
because who ultimately knows themselves, their cell-free soul

Intertextual Flythroughs

Tissue per tissue
mind per mind
by listening to the sounds
of hummers gone by
I was just a larva when I started becoming me

I am a sound-built mind on its travels
Extra sounds enrich my life
wherever I listen to them

A word of caution though: build yourself only from sounds
that take you toward something good
Forget about the unexplored and unfaithful ones
Listen to the sound of your soul
Let it fuel you on your way upward

Without the other female and male bumblebees
including the queen mother, my father, my descendants
I wouldn't be here
Apart from my father, I let the ears of the others burn
Utilizing swarm intelligence
can lead to toughness, useful awareness, pure uselessness,
not unlike the narratives of society
But as with choosing the male, one must filter the information,
consider the resource and intertexts

Together in a Colony

One wingstroke at a time I begin to bring my dreams to life
A fantasy turned into a dream, a dream into goals, a goal into
reality

I didn't get to dance the courtship dance, maybe you were
obliged to the first time around?
Now that it's a new life
could we dance the courtship dance
study new age-old ways
to show the colony
that it's us buzzing together

I should wrap things up
to avoid hitting the window

Can love make a bumblebee burst?
Maybe but I won't do anything so irresponsible

My Melting Mind

My mind melted into you
I need to keep its fire burning
I have failed to realize
how fragile my heart is
how quick it is to open up
and
melt
accept the desire it's dealt

I hope you are ready
won't spin me on a spit
inspect from angles
stick a fork in me
add to the dripping

I'm fragile already
I don't need a savior
but a bearer of
what's left of the roast

I'm trying to stay strong
pliable
unscorchable
I can take one more moment
of waiting
whether you'll recognize me

Although I fear
I melted already
my heartrate off the charts
Please don't fear
like I do
Just melt!

Humming Is Only Humming?

I've arrived at the nest
It's time to meet up
Be his
I'm his
Dreaming takes us there

One more moment I'll live behind my time
my dreaming turning into real
touching
but to be me and to be you
we also need constant humming
for that's what our souls are made of

My faith is strong
and though I'm still dreaming
I keep my bumblebee feet on the ground
If we get tired before the nest
it's all right, as long as we'll survive on stock syrup
that sure is cause enough for joy
Although who in this time in eternity would not choose
fulfillment,
home base and love, you
But even if one gets that
every relationship is always coming to an end, whether
through separation or death
In the end there are only two dualistic alternatives:
from joy to sorrow or sorrow to joy

Be that as it may, it's nothing major when it's just about the
two of us
Let's not sink into pessimism but do things, small ones to
begin reviving the colony
I want to be an optimist
Will you join me?
Will ya be mine?

After Melt Waters

After the melting process
the melt waters have flowed into ditches, rivers, bays
there's one and another thing

Even though we vibrate on the same level with small ones or
big ones really
some secrets I'd like to keep to us

Cryptically humming on open channels
do remind me later on that I have something to say about
opposites burned by polarization
I've realized what the meaning of the ability to mirror is
How the hard break, the flexible bend
you will get to buzz and fuss about the grief with me

Maybe the wonders of bumblebeeness open roads to freedom
even though looking for and lynching scapegoats is the junk of
vanity fairs
But if we take the road to clarity together, it will free up
cognitive capital and make it flow greener energy

In the summer it is wonderful to fly and vibrate and let light
wingstrokes touch you lightly

The Weak and the Strong Stand Out

Us bumblebees are a versatile bunch
One breaks down by looking inward
and breaks down
even without looking
if they can't accept the help available

Another one looks inward
understands themself
if they don't come up with a cure
they realize there's help out there
and grow stronger through that
offer support for others

Yet none of these
can be put up on a pedestal
because both of them
have been given a role
at birth already
with minor fixes done in childhood
and final touches in youth

If only parents would remember
to let their larva shine
would not neglect or lash at them even
when a sensitive one is provoking or bullying others
whether it be about eopupa, eopupae, pupae, pupas, though
not puppies
Would see, make visible
Would pull close at a moment of closeness
and be vibrating: how are ya doing?

That way a metamorphosis would result in
an adult breaking out of their pupa cell
one that adjusts
one that survives in life

On the Sauna Window

I fly onto the sauna window, stay there to heat up, enjoy
Although I'm a little bumblebee
I'm old already
and it's come down to being strong
To understand
that the brightness of my black-and-yellow stripes
the hairiness of my legs
the symmetry and size of my head
the sensuality of my mouthparts and eyes
do not define me
I am good or I am bad
and my looks neither worsen or improve that

But let it be so
that the young ones get to strut their stuff
treasure their beauty
as long as they remember
the sooner they grow out of it
the healthier they will feel
And if beauty is a value
let it be a floating one
So that the honey of the colony
will provide a floating place for anybody

And in case of a deep internal need
it's okay with some minor surgery
except for down there
because happiness is accepting oneself
not avoiding to fulfill one's mission

One must remember
that vibrating makes it possible
to build the world
in one way or another
Despite the shape of the body
you can choose
to look at yourself with acceptance
or hoping to be something else

Looking with affection
will turn you into your friend
who accepts your desire
but understands it to be
distortion created by others

The harmonization of our dissimilarity is no longer needed
when we accept ourselves and each other
as we are

You/I Are/Am Valuable

You don't have to come crawling to me
or anyone else
Just be proud of yourself
you have reason to

You have soaked yourself
in filthy waters
You have flown
in fiery nests
You haven't got to where you are
without a fight
Therefore: let your lovely black-and-yellow fur vibrate
Puff, strut it out in no hurry, my love
I'm proud of you

But please be proud of me too
and always root for me
for though I make myself smaller
I'm equally proud without showing it
It requires a level of skill
to fly in a swarm
without rising too high
so that others will also feel good
and they won't out of jealousy
fly away from the support network

The Power of Honey

That sugary stuff
that many gather enough
to feed themselves and their larvae
Gatherers, those diligent workers
should be
proud of themselves
There is no job more important
than the gathering of honey

It's no use envying the ones
that gather more than they need and process it
sell their honey to other colonies
Business is business
and with such short flights
it's also green

The few pennies that they make
are not for one to take
but the colony does stand
its networks to expand
if only the politicians would understand
that honey can't rival a friendship's band

One should watch out for greediness
because it easily leads to speed blindness
money becoming more valuable than time
only leads to crime
Even worse is to start
a war because of it
If only the bumblebees of the tyrant-led tsarist nation would get
this

Competition Hums to the Leader

Although rules can sometimes shackle
they stabilize the activities of a colony
as long as they are being followed

Some also regard colony rules in an overly sacred way
They are tough
Some thrive
Some burn out
Some step aside
Which too can be wise
Unless it is the most talented one
and what a loss that is for the colony

Let us remember: the rules apply to everyone
Consider what is fair based on the level
Favoring is acceptable only on the top level if even then
And the lower down we are buzzing
would it be impossible to understand:
Some mature later
Some are the underachievers

Yet in colonies and the colonies of colonies
we need competition
rules
good leaders
who understand the feelings of little bumblebees

To understand don't just listen but internalize
Look in the mirror

In the absence of memos
don't think that there's no whining in the nest
Open the channel

Don't play games behind the back
Even little bumblebees tend to get it
that without understanding and forgiveness from the leader
unhappy hums start going around

Be a listener and trust until proven otherwise by action
Even then give a second chance maybe two
So there's no bitterness
for processes are cumulative coils

You should turn wisdoms like these askew
if the leader is evil like a tyrant, whether a tsar or an emperor
which makes the strength of the colony shrink

The Underachiever's Time

When's the time for the underachiever to celebrate?
That time can come so very late

She's resting in the confines of the nest
protecting herself
against pressures
put on her by herself or others
real or imagined ones

The hard rules of the game she can accept
but she might not realize or know
how to make herself grow
because the mind is buffering against that too
The insurgent bumblebee has chosen a good path:
this way she can forge her own way
toward unforeseen, novel worlds

Sometimes it might be better
that failures would teach us less about other things than the
one being studied
At the same time nothing is more didactic
than learning through mistakes

Probably the best thing
would be to choose one's way of learning:
underachievement, flawless performance or overachievement
Where to find an employer, leader, educator, trainer
who'd identify
who is who
and point one on a suitable path to fly
This is easy
once you understand the disposition of the control-resisting
underachiever
and if and only if the path is inspected from multiple
perspectives

Will You Irritate Me?

The journey toward self-acceptance can begin
from identifying an irritating feature in someone else

Ask yourself
what irritates you
Do you see something
that you admire
but don't possess yourself
like appropriateness or vice versa: silliness

Why do we so often admire
what we don't have
Is that the way to keep a bumblebee's insecurity a constant?

And if you identify the feature in your partner
it's time to ask
who's actually the one making the relationship more stable or
fun perhaps
whatever it is that you want:
a controlled way of flying
or having foolish fun after all

Recognizing the irritation can neutralize it
It is the only way toward accepting dissimilarity
that lives both in ourselves and others
and
when we get there
we grow deeper relationships with ourselves, others, even
trees

By crossing this abyss we start to get even more in love with
ourselves and others and trees and furries

I promise to love your irritating features the most
even though it requires a conscious effort

Do hum about this in the home base:
What puts whom on the fence?
This will discharge the energy of difference
give dualism some sense

Through our senses
we buzz to address anxiety in our relationship or colony
and our lives become free from anxiety
Then and only then is it possible to avoid solutions
that rip relationships apart
as by themselves

Do fight for your relationship though:
don't look for a guilty party in or outside of it
recognize difficulties
take responsibility
make your own decisions
even without the master present
and without thinking how they'd solve the issue
or without imagining how an imagined change would solve the
issue[1]
Remember
bad solutions may be more important than
stalling, havering and wavering

We have reason to ban the phrases that mitigate our feelings
in our colony:
we should not deny our feelings to deal with them
paying attention to them makes us most organized

---

[1] Nikkola, T. (2011). *Oppimisen esteet ja mahdollisuudet ryhmässä. Syyllisyyden kehittyminen syntipukki-ilmiöksi opiskeluryhmässä ohjaajan tulkitsemana.* University of Jyväskylä. Retrieved 2022-09-27 from http://urn.fi/URN:ISBN:978-951-39-4505-3

Let us proclaim the beginning of centuries of feelings
Let us pronounce anxiety as the new super power
let the power churn
the world upside down turn
for the wellbeing of all little bumblebees out there

Let us forget about the unnecessary evils
leave the waters and the nectars
eat dust and honey
scrape by, freeze, harden ourselves

How else to paperlessly buzz or swap honey on the
blockchains
with the flame burning tame?
The solution can hardly be the distancing of the colonies from
each other
unless we extend it all the way to substancelessness?
I vibrate

Perhaps the idiocy of the tyrant has provided the other
colonies with a solution:
the patronization of addictions should be reserved only
for those with a sense of justice
The only thing left is the preservation of historical facts and
relative realities
buzzing about those and present experiences cherishing
freedom with that for that if anything will prevent polarization

On the Open Sea

Catastrophes shimmer in my eyes
from just thinking about ships
And I cannot from my fears flee
because I live by the sea
I will share an even more terrible tale now
than when Titanic or Estonia sank down

Once upon a time a ship sailed on the open sea
pushing against the wind with its sails
but now ploughing through the sea
is a teeny-weeny plastic flake people
born out of the pressure of the Earth
there evolving into big black innovoil
that I would like nothing to do with ever again

And these people do not discuss
or negotiate
but insidiously inch their way
like the KGB does
into cells

Of small animals
such as bumblebees
Large hawks
The kings of the forests
Poor human beings

The cell will soon be full
of the nest-like noise
that splits the head
and causes dread

How much DNA does a cell contain?
Soon the DNA will be void of the plump red blood cells
of legally donatable blood
disk-like nucleus-free platelets
plasma from antibodies
and left with cold eternal
plastic waste

Even though I faced my fears
by planning my own funeral,
the life of one little bumblebee
is not very significant
in the cosmic scheme of things

And even though I hate cleaning,
it's time to mention
that there are few more valuable tasks
than bearing the responsibility for worthless messes

Not only must one clean their own nest
but also
the seas out of the plastic
gases out of the rooms
metallic debris out of space
antibiotic factories out of the heedless east

Why is cleaning so very difficult?
Who could keep it up?

An Ode to Sensible Standardization

Sometimes I shift
from fantasies to pondering
over a paperless planet
where machines are clattering
battering their two digits
and taking detours to ruin the air
Every single time you turn the machine on
Did you know that?

Is it time to start
using blurred images
when the natural ones are always more beautiful
and build lower-bit sites
with fewer pages
as a logical system of concepts

Is it time
to standardize software
by terminologizing them multilingually – or at least in Finnish ;)
Despite the brand and colors changing
one wouldn't have to learn a formatted application from
scratch

Is it time
to ditch the blockchains
if we can't make them more workable
For godssake they're no good
for storing and supplying honey

Is it time to standardize programming languages too
Don't we know by now
how to get the job done with less clattering

Who would invent
a solution to forget or at least downscale the socials
to focus on getting one good picture to capture and publicize
a moment
to have it immortalized in the mind of a bumblebee
Whether an instant or a long-term moment, it's absurd
that it gets replicated on numerous routes
Even a website is more logical
than five different social media accounts for each bumblebee

What if we move from the time of individuality to creating
collective content?
From headshots to faceless images?

And the bumblebees would start buzzing in the yards and their
nests instead of networks
that produce no honey but much humming
that turn relationships to shallow drumming

What makes a little bumblebee think about such things
Oh hell if I know
Couldn't a bigger shot
take on pushing honey treasures to researchers
And if so taken and pushed
I guess it means
that the world already is better than yesterday?

Before Substancelessness

Hanging onto this time
yet with a terrible handicap
please remember
to put together a time strategy with me

I'm not bitter about any past moment
although to be honest I could have left a couple of things
undone

But on a floating surface our shanks quickly tread too many
steps in places
with only vanity to experience
or what's even worse is
we're floating apart from each other
secretly drifting further away from one another

Oy, I'm again announcing the need for awareness!
Without awareness our time is broken into pieces
but by proceeding strategically
tactically at times
waving the trump cards when need be
we can accumulate our time in the right direction

Our sprint is so strong
and it no longer matters
that at the moment of departure
we weren't young
we still have life to live
to win in the perfect way
though we must remember the antithesis:
life is wonderful in its ordinariness and roughness

On the Common Colony Market

There are colonies
and
then there are colonies
Lousier, better

Lousier queens, workers, males
or better
Buzzes, encounters, nests, routes, the same story, often
stationary, even accumulative

How could the colonies of our world accelerate onto a path of
evolution?
Not by hiding the nectar in the stump for sure
Or by making war
Rather by strengthening each bumblebee's entrepreneurship
and by loving

Many solutions have been found:
protect the bumblebees
eat insects
consume responsibly
live economically
use quilts and sweaters
don't hoard too much space
learn to live close to others again and in peace

For increased happiness the fourth route will strengthen and
globalization weaken
Markets will fragment again
products become simpler
With enrichments & accompaniments available in jars
With no imported meat, watermelon, banana, passion fruit or
other unnecessary passions from across the world

Let's lower ourselves to eat
what grows on our land
Let us lower ourselves together!

At the Focal Point of the Irreal and the Real

You might have your doubts
if you saw my buzz
I'm a serious bumblebee

It took me nearly half a century to realize
that I do have feelings
Sometimes they're just unrecognizable
or maybe that was the case in my youth
that I just grew out of
that I can't go back to

How can a bumblebee have two sides
so distant from each other
My everyday life is in the real world
accepting even its gritty realism
though dreading to share it
pulling through with dark humor and laughter
I'm in my nest in my nest

Just this search for a male messing with my head
but I'll pull through that too
A life without obstacles is no life

My love
Please come to me
when the moment is right
Let's join in all the things that feel good
and all the rest
we can solve out of death's way asap asap

A Notice from the Queen to All Bumblebee Females and Males

When you set out
wherever you are going
you should look carefully into the matter
Reading makes you wiser
believe the researcher
And not only researched knowledge
but small tips stories bumblebees buzz to each other
whether fictional or factual

Pay attention now!
Do not dispute the information
especially if your mind is immediately opposed to its reception
On the contrary
that's when it's time to examine
what your mind wants you to imagine
This likely happens to everyone at times
but the ones who should watch out
are all the introverts flying around with open minds

Perhaps your mind is trying to spare you
from a distressing feeling
But especially then
simply by facing that feeling
can you benefit and learn from your intuition

One more wisdom I would like to utter to you as your queen
not all knowledge can be acquired by reading facts
If you wish to learn about love
forget about your pride and abandon your prejudice about it as
vain humbug

Instead
assume a relaxed flying position
and follow a romantic movie
or while reaping the harvest
stop to read a book
your hearing organs feeling the night's wishes
Let the story touch you
whatever it may be humming to you

I Believe

I believe
that I would be your match
I could support you
Be your equal in many ways

But if this is not going not happen
it comes with its upsides
I will of course be saddened by
us not buzzing, humming, vibrating, trembling for each other
That we won't be us

But I notice when thinking about
whether I really am good enough like this
I shrink and I think which hums I'll let you miss

Perhaps we were really
no soulmates ideally
There's no way of knowing without trying
I would have been ready
even though you weren't

There's a bit of hope left
I can only wait
Although I am mentally prepared for my defeat
my faith will not change it one way or another
for my thoughts will not change reality, only humming has the
power to do that

Suddenly it hit me
I have to let go
Not completely but of ownership
I can't use my thoughts, will to control him
He will show up if he wants to

Maybe you can let go piece by piece?
It's not quite time to let go completely
But if it comes to it
I'm ready for it too

Because soulmates commit to a suitable
fragmented whole
where a part of my part settles in place
and a part is left crooked
If only you could divide the males into poly pieces
pick and choose the lovely parts
But that would not be experiencing real love
where even the shitty parts will do

My Final Buzzes to You

Do remember
you don't have to be perfect
You will still be perfect to me
if only you understand to give into a female's love

You can no longer be the male
flying only on routes of his own
You cannot avoid listening
when I ask you to slow down
if I see
that your speed has blinded you

If you don't give into love
you will miss that what makes you strong as a male
is not always getting your way
but
seeing inward too

When you do you will
share your strength with us
the diverse yet your very own foolish, smart, sometimes
anxious, sometimes enthusiastic bunch of bumblebees

And if you remain a substanceless speculation
there will be the bumblebee devil to pay
For the strongest of faiths can miss
if humming comes with no gifts
like kisses blown
or services required without axes thrown

But life is
what it is
and
in every world
the one who seeks finds a path or two
I too will:
find a suitable one
And if I don't
I'll picture the path
to be my soul's aftermath

And what a life it will be!
I smile and keep going

Author

Heli Katajamäki (born Lähteenmaa in 1973) grew up as a child of a factory community in the most famous village of Finland, Koskenkorva, where the liquor by the same name is distilled. Like many other villagers, her grandfather Erkki and father Matti worked in the factory, and even Heli was employed there as a laboratory assistant for one  summer. She currently resides in the town of Isokyrö, also known for its distillery, the Kyrö Distillery. Therefore, she can still attribute her goofiness to falling into a pot still.

After graduating from Ilmajoki High School, Heli started studying mathematics at the University of Helsinki. However, instead of working hard to do well in her studies, she opted to switch study paths. She left Helsinki for Vaasa after being admitted to the University of Vaasa to study Modern Finnish and Communication Studies. She earned her master's degree in 1998, licentiate's degree in 2005, and doctoral degree in Applied Linguistics in 2018. In 2000, she received her pedagogical qualification from the Jyväskylä School of Professional Teacher Education. Her research focuses on language for specific purposes, critical discourse analysis, systemic functional linguistics, attitude theory, and terminology theory. In addition to language and communication, Heli has always been interested in social issues, such as politics, economics, or whatever might have inspired her at a given time, and she has held office in various roles in the Trade Union for Education, OAJ, for more than 15 years.

Heli has three children (born 1997, 2003, and 2011). Since the beginning of 2022, she has unleashed her creativity by being immersed in theories and practices of love affairs. Heli is seeking to make the world a better place – like so many of us – which is an important message of this book. As we all know, the greatest force for saving the world is love.

Currently, Heli works as a University Lecturer in Finnish Language and Communication at the University of Vaasa Language Centre Linginno. Besides teaching, she is working on research articles and editing VAKKI Publications together with colleagues.

Instagram & Twitter: @helsuskat
ResearchGate & LinkedIn: Heli Katajamäki

Instagram & Twitter: @helsuskat
ResearchGate & LinkedIn: Heli Katajamäki

Translator (*Buzzing Like a Bumblebee*)

Susanna Rönn (born 1980) has been an avid writer since the age of eight, and started dreaming of a career as a translator while in elementary school. At the tender age of 16, she moved from her childhood home in Peräseinäjoki to Vaasa to attend the International Baccalaureate high school. Susanna calls Vaasa her home, although she has also spent years living in the United States and our dear neighboring country of Sweden.

In 2009, Susanna earned her Master of Arts degree from the University of Vaasa, where she studied English and Modern Finnish. She has almost 20 years of experience working as a translator. She has translated mostly commercial and technical texts, as well as audiovisual material from English and Swedish into Finnish and vice versa.

Currently, Susanna works as a University Teacher at the University of Vaasa Language Centre Linginno, teaching Finnish and English. She also finds time to work on her dissertation in Communication Studies, write crime fiction for her own pleasure, go to rock concerts, and wander the many jogging trails of her hometown. She lives in Vaasa with her two daughters.

Instagram: @electricsuzy80
Academia.edu & LinkedIn: Susanna Rönn

Translator (*Hummelgesumm*)

Tiina Sorvali (born 1962) has translated the book into German. Tiina considers herself an amateur translator, but that has not kept her from teaching courses in translation.

Originally from Eastern Finland, Tiina spent her school years in the province of Häme and studied at the University of Helsinki (MA in 1991) and the University of Tampere (LA in 1997, PhD in 2004). Her studies consisted of German and English philology, educational science, adult education, and other random topics of interest. Life has taken this girl from the east of Finland around the country and parts of Europe, having lived in Scotland, Sweden, and, of course, Germany for periods of time. Since 2005, Tiina has lived in Vaasa and worked as a University Lecturer in German at the University of Vaasa Language Centre. Tiina loves Rammstein, rock, and raw metaphors.

Twitter: @TiiKarhu
Instagram: @tiinasorvali

Illustrator

Heta Kettunen (born 1989), the illustrator of the book, comes from Vaasa. At a young age, she developed an interest in games and videogames that led her to study audiovisual communication (media assistant) at the Vaasa Vocational Institute.

Heta was also interested in airplanes to the extent that in 2010, while in the army in Jämsä, she completed the Noncommissioned Officer Course in Flight Engineering  (assistant mechanic). However, Heta found aircraft technology too challenging and continued her studies at Teesside University in Middlesbrough, England. In 2014, she earned her Bachelor of Arts degree in Computer Games Art. After graduation, she started working for Nitro Games in Kotka, where she is still employed as a creator of characters and graphics. As a side job, Heta designs graphics for the Bureau of Creative Agents. Heta lives in Vantaa with her partner and shiba inu dog. She enjoys taking walks in the forest (especially to look for mushrooms!), running, and playing videogames, of course.

Instagram: @hetakettu

The Inseparable Fate of Bumblebees and Human Beings

Eero Vartiainen
D.Sc. (Tech.) and a beekeeper's son

Bumblebees (*Bombus*) are a genus of species of winged insects that belong to one of the bee families, *Apidae*[1]. They are part of the same bee superfamily, *Apoidea*, as the well-known western honey bee (*Apis mellifera*)[2]. The most important role of bumblebees in the ecosystem is the pollination of seed plants, which is essential for the reproduction of plants, except for self-pollinating plants like oat, wheat, and barley[3].

Bumblebees are excellent pollinators, as they only feed on flowers and visit them industriously. Unlike honey bees, they travel even in cloudy and cool weathers, including slightly freezing temperatures. The most important flowers that bumblebees pollinate in Finland are blueberries, lingonberries, raspberries, and fruit trees. Bumblebees favor blue, purple, and red flowers.[1]

Bumblebees are eusocial insects that form colonies of a few tens or hundreds of individuals. A single queen establishes a new nest in a pre-existing cavity, such as a birdhouse, lining it with moss, grass, and feathers. A nest usually lasts for a single season and is led by a mother capable of reproduction. The workers (females) of the nest take care of the it and collect flower nectar to feed the colony. The only role of the drones (males) is to mate with the new mother of another nest. They do not contribute to the feeding of the nest.[1]

The Love Life of Bumblebees

The young bumblebee queen mates at the age of five days. Drones leave seductive scent marks on the ground or vegetation and remain waiting nearby either on or above the ground, or by the opening to the nest. As the queen arrives at the scent mark, the drone will lead her aside for mating. The queen will only mate with one drone, and the mating takes place in the morning, taking 10 to 90 minutes. Over the winter, the sperms are stored in the queen's spermatheca, a chamber for the sperms. Using her wax glands, the queen builds pupae for the larvae hatching from the eggs. She keeps the larvae warm with her body, staying in the nest after laying the eggs. To thwart competition, the queen secretes a pheromone that prevents workers from laying eggs.[1]

Image. Bombus impatiens (Insects Unlocked, CC0).

After mating, the young bumblebee queen digs a hibernation hole for herself, typically settling in it in August, prior to the cooling of the weather. After the queen abandons the nest to hibernate, it deteriorates, and the workers and drones die, as the weather turns freezing. The queen stays in diapause over the winter, using the stores of fat and glycogen in the posterior part of her body to produce glycerol to keep her from freezing. After a diapause of eight to nine months, the queen is ready to build a new nest in the spring.[1]

The Disappearing Pollinators

The number of winged insects and pollinators, in particular, has
plummeted in recent years[4]. In Germany, the insect mass has been
calculated to have decreased by 75 percent in the last 27 years[5].The
previously common species of Cullum's bumblebee (*Bombus
cullumanus*), for instance, is disappearing in Europe with over 40
percent of pollinator insects on the brink of regional extinction[4].
Because 70 to 80 percent of plants need pollinators[6], the change is
highly alarming both for animal and human nutrition. In France, the
rural bird population has fallen by a third in the last 17 years because
of the decrease in insects for nutrition[7]. In Finland Proper, rape crops
have decreased by a third in 15 years.[6]

For humans, the most significant consequence of the disappearance
of pollinators may be nutrient imbalance. Approximately 90 percent
of vitamin C, almost all antioxidants, and most of vitamin A come
from insect-pollinated plants[6,7]. It has been estimated that over two
billion people will suffer from vitamin A deficiency[8]. Iron deficiency
leads to anemia and calcium deficiency to weakened bones[6]. The
reasons for pollinators disappearing are not fully known but are most
likely related to pesticide use in plant cultivation, invasive alien
species, habitat reduction, and climate change[4]. The prevention of
climate change is vital also for pollinators. The fates of bumblebees
and human beings truly are inseparably connected.

References

Literature

1. Bumblebee [Internet]. Retrieved 2022-09-27 from
   https://en.wikipedia.org/wiki/Bumblebee
2. Bee [Internet]. Retrieved 2022-09-27 from
   https://en.wikipedia.org/wiki/Bee
3. Pollination [Internet]. Retrieved 2022-09-27 from
   https://en.wikipedia.org/wiki/Pollination
4. Asikainen, H. [Internet]. Pölyttäjien määrä on romahtanut – ja siitä voi
   tulla ihmiskunnan kohtalonkysymys. *YLE* 2020. Retrieved 2022-09-27
   from https://yle.fi/aihe/artikkeli /2020/04 /01/polyttajien-maara-on-
   romahtanut-ja-siita-voi-tulla-ihmiskunnan-kohtalonkysymys
5. Hallmann, C., Sorg, M., Jongejans, E. et al. More than 75% decline over
   27 years in total flying insect biomass in protected areas. *PLoS One*
   2017. Retrieved 2022-09-27 from
   https://journals.plos.org/plosone/article?id=10.1371
   /journal.pone.0185809
6. Hokkanen, H., Menzler-Hokkanen, I. & Hokkanen, S.. Mitä tapahtuu jos
   pölyttäjät katoavat? *Lääketieteellinen aikakauskirja Duodecim* 2018;
   134(13):1321–4. Retrieved 2022-09-27 from
   https://www.duodecimlehti.fi/duo14408
7. Geoffrey, L. [Internet]. Where have all the farmland birds gone? *CNRS*
   2018. Retrieved 2022-09-27 from https://news.cnrs.fr/articles/where-
   have-all-the-farmland-birds-gone
8. Smith, M., Singh, G., Mozaraffian, D. et al. Effects of decreases of
   animal pollinators on human nutrition and global health: a modelling
   analysis. *Lancet* 2015; 386:1964–72.

Images

Almbauer, Marco, CC0, via Wikimedia Commons;
   https://upload.wikimedia.org/wikipedia/commons/c/c0/Bombus_terrest
   ris_head_in_detail.jpg
Insects Unlocked, CC0, via Wikimedia Commons;
   https://upload.wikimedia.org/wikipedia/commons/9/9e/Bombus_impati
   ens_%2822659635111%29.jpg

Image. Bombus terrestris (Almbauer, CC0)

The fates of bumblebees and human beings
are inseparably connected.

Heli Susanna Katajamäki's buzzes
narrate not only the lives, colonies, and surroundings of
bumblebees but also a little bumblebee's longing for that
special someone.

The bumblebee's sharp, insightful observations lead us to
basic questions about life – a loveless life is a wasted life for
bumblebees and human beings alike. Reading the buzzes
clears the mind and nourishes the soul – not to mention the
many moments of joy and melancholy.

Eero Vartiainen